Musings,

Magic,

and Mischief

A collection of short stories and poems

By Stacey Broadbent

Published by Stacey Broadbent, Ashburton, NZ
Copyright 2023 © Stacey Broadbent

Licence Notes

Proofreading by Spell Bound
Cover image from Deposit Photos
Cover Design by Stacey Broadbent

ISBN: 978-0-473-67588-2 (paperback)
         978-0-473-67589-9 (kindle)
         978-0-473-68307-8 (IngramSpark paperback)

Musings,

Magic,

and Mischief

A collection of short stories and poems

By Stacey Broadbent

Dedicated to

The Ashburton Writers' Group

To the wonderful members who keep me on my toes, inspire me to be better, and keep me entertained of an evening. You challenge and encourage me, and it means the world to me.

Contents

Introduction

Hello, and thank you for picking up a copy of my book, *Musings, Magic, and Mischief.* This is the third book in the *Musings of a Writer* series, and each has been a labour of love.

Writing has always been an outlet for me, even from a young age, but it wasn't until around seven years ago that I decided to give it a go as something more than just putting my emotions on paper. I started out with one story and no intentions of going further, but then something clicked inside, and my brain kept conjuring stories and I couldn't write fast enough to keep up!

It was a happy accident that I discovered the Ashburton Writers' Group, which helped me find another outlet for those incessant stories. I was contacted by the secretary and asked to come along and talk about my process with the group, and after meeting them all, I ended up joining on the spot. We have monthly assignments, and these can often be a challenge, but I like that it forces me to think outside my norm, as well as learning to keep stories to the word limit allocated.

In this book you'll find a number of those assignments (both in story and poem form), plus some I wrote for competitions or just for fun.

As with the previous *Musings of a Writer* collections, you'll find a wee snippet at the end of each story/poem to tell you the inspiration or prompt behind it.

I hope you enjoy this collection.

Stacey xxx

Stacey Broadbent

The Dancer

Hushed voices, darkened room
Curling nice and small.
Almost there, nearly time
Trundling down the hall.
Door opens, shouts abound
Laughter off the wall.
Wheels squeak, music blares
It's my curtain call.
Lid lifts, bursting forth
Time to bare it all.
Bikini clad, heels strapped on
Feeling six feet tall.
Cheers erupt, clapping hands
Confetti starts to fall.
Hips gyrating, body shaking
On the floor I crawl.
Raining money, making bank
Collecting quite a haul.
Happy birthday, Mr. Man
I hope you have a ball.

The Dancer was written as part of an assignment entitled "write about an incident that could be used against you if you ever ran for political office". It took me a while to come up with this one, as I kept drawing a blank. I finally decided to go with an exotic dancer turned politician as it always seems to be some sort of sordid/sexual activity that they get caught up in. I pictured the dancer leaping out of one of those birthday cakes and entertaining the guests.

Happy Thoughts

"MY MARBLES. Have you seen them?" Tootles asked as he tossed another cushion across the room. "I've searched everywhere, and I can't find them." He sniffled, swiping an angry hand across his eyes. "I could've sworn I left them right there." He pointed at the tree stump in the centre of the room. They used this as a table when playing cards in the evenings.

"Sorry, Tootles, I haven't seen them. But I can help you look," Wendy offered, dropping to her knees and peering beneath the worn armchair in the corner.

"Thanks, Wendy." His voice waivered, overcome with grief. "I can't fly without them." A sob burst from his lips, and he buried his face in his hands.

"Oh, Tootles," Wendy gushed, rushing over to wrap him in her arms. "Whatever do you mean? Marbles can't make you fly." She frowned, realising it was no sillier to believe in the fairy dust they all used. After all, this was Neverland, and anything was possible.

Tootles pulled away from her embrace, resting on his haunches. "But they *do*, Wendy. *Mine* do." His lips twisted to the side. "They're where I keep my happy thoughts."

"Oh." That was a problem then. You needed fairy dust *and* happy thoughts to fly. "But can't you think of some new happy thoughts?" She scoured the room then quickly snatched up a tiny pebble. "You could think of one thing right now and store it in here." She smiled, holding her hand out flat with the pebble on her palm.

Tootles frowned. "You can't keep happy thoughts in a stone, Wendy." His tone suggested it was a ridiculous notion.

Her hand fell to her lap, the pebble rolling to the floor. As she stooped to pick it up, she caught sight of something glinting.

"Wait a second…" Lying flat on her stomach, she wiggled beneath the couch, all the way to the back. A fluffy bear and a dirty sock were tucked away in the corner, and there, poking out from behind the bear's bottom, was a marble. She plucked it out and sent it rolling towards Tootles, followed by four more.

"Oh, Wendy!" he exclaimed, jumping to his feet. "You found them! You found my happy thoughts!"

As she shimmied her way back out, Tootles leapt into the air, his eyes closed, and his hand held in a tight fist. He zoomed to the ceiling and did a circuit of the room before landing down beside her. "Thank you, Wendy. Thank you for finding my marbles."

Happy Thoughts was written for an assignment where we were to start a story with a character who has lost something important to them. Peter Pan is a favourite childhood story, and I adored the movie adaptation, Hook. Of course, as soon as I heard the assignment, I instantly thought of Tootles and his missing marbles.

Shadow for the Day

Come and be my shadow,
If only for a day.
Follow in my footsteps,
And hear the things I say.
Up with the sun each morning,
And off out for a walk.
It's the perfect time for thinking;
There's no need to talk.

Now it's time for breakfast;
A piece of toast is fine.
Then drop the children off at school,
Watch them join the line.
Head off to the office,
Where messages await.
A manuscript to edit;
I'm up to chapter eight.

Working through the lunch break;
I need to push on through.
Another job is waiting;
In three days it is due.
Stopping for a coffee,
I open Photoshop.
I need to make some cute adverts
To make my pages pop.

Lost inside a rabbit hole
Of images and memes.
I can't decide which one to choose,
And I'm about to scream.
I scroll until my eyes do blur;
The pictures look the same.
How is one supposed to know
Which one will end in fame?

And then I must remember
To find some time to write,
That pesky little story,
That keeps me up at night.
Opening the file,
I wish for inspiration.
My brain of course refuses;
I've no imagination.

Closing down the laptop,
I heave a hefty sigh.
I'll leave it for tomorrow.
At least I gave a try.
The day is almost over,
And look what I've achieved;
No ending for my story.
No cover to be sleeved.

This was an assignment from my early days in the group, with the prompt *Shadow for the Day*. I literally take you on a journey of a typical day in my life – where I can don the hat of mother, editor, author, cover designer, and housewife.

Uninvited

"WHAT DO YOU THINK OF PURPLE? Or maybe pink?" I ask, fluffing my hair with my hand. "I've always wanted to try those colours."

"Ooh, you'd really suit purple. Do you want me to help? I'm actually qualified, would you believe?" Tabitha chuckles, zipping up her suitcase and extending the handle. She pulls it along behind her as we walk towards her car.

"You are? What are you doing here then?" I wave my hand at the Nail Tech building we just left.

"I want a salon that offers both hair and nails." She grins. "It's all part of my master plan."

"Of course. I forgot about that." The first day of class, Tabitha had sat at the table beside me, introduced herself, and then proceeded to explain her five-year plan. I had been suitably impressed. Four years my junior, and she has her whole life planned out, while I can barely manage to plan my meals for the week, let along my next five years.

"I might even have some purple dye at home. You should come over this weekend." She tugs at the hair hanging around my face. "I've been dying to get my hands on these greys since day one." She grins, stopping at her car. "Come around tomorrow morning, okay? And bring that hunky boyfriend of yours."

I nod, waving my hand, when inside I'm still trying to process what she said.

She's been dying to get her hands on my *greys*? My hand moves to my hair. What greys? I'm only 26. I don't have grey hair!

I climb into my car and pull onto the road. My eyes keep flicking up to the rearview mirror, trying to catch a glimpse of the greys she's talking about, but all I see is blonde.

Back at home, I switch the light in the bathroom on and peer at my reflection. I twist side-to-side, and there, above my ear, is a thick strand of silver hair. And another farther back on my head, and even more towards my temple. In fact, there are loads of them slotted in between the fine blonde strands.

I stare in horror as my fingers pull out more and more of the offending strands. When did this happen? How long have they been there? I don't remember inviting these intruders onto my head. I'm not even thirty yet!

I bet it started when Tabitha noticed Darryl, my boyfriend, one afternoon after class. He'd come to pick me up, and the next morning, Tabitha had practically frothed at the mouth telling me how hot he was. It had been a little disturbing, but I'd put it behind me and moved on, even forming a friendship of sorts with her. But now… Now I had grey hairs to thank her for. And she had the audacity to point them out to me.

Bracing my hands on the sink, I gape at the coarse hairs I've gathered, and another unpleasant thought occurs to me. Pulling my lips between my teeth, I step back from the sink, grab hold of my waistband, and pull it away from me. The elastic pings against my skin as my fingers lose grip and I stumble backwards. "No," I whisper. "No, no, no." This can't be happening.

With tweezers in hand, I tug the fabric of my pants down again and pluck the shining hair from my nether regions. I add it to the pile of hairs in the sink and turn the tap on, washing away all evidence of my uninvited guests.

Uninvited was an assignment titled "the uninvited guest", and though it's not where most people's mind would instantly go, mine went to a particular memory of mine from when I was training to be a nail technician. One of the girls in class had continually told me how attractive my fiancé was, and then proceeded to tell me how she wanted to attack my greys, which I was completely oblivious to. Thus, *Uninvited* was born.

The Writer

Weaving magic with only words,
A writer's voice can be heard,
Turning phrases to describe,
All the world seen from their eyes.

Painting pictures you can see,
Drawing from a memory.
Images of childhood fun,
Of finding faith; seeing the sun.

What you see inside your head,
Is but an image they have led,
With perfectly descriptive prose,
So you can see what they propose.

And that, dear reader, you will find,
Is what pushes the writer's mind.
For an author's voice needs only this;
To send their reader into bliss.

The writer was another assignment. This one was to simply write a poem, and as it was a writing assignment, I felt it appropriate to use that as my muse. I'm really enjoying getting back into poetry. It's something I dabbled with as a child and young adult, and up until joining Ashburton Writers' Group, I've rediscovered my love for them.

Time to Wake

A LOUD OBNOXIOUS SOUND, almost like a siren, blears from somewhere nearby. "Shit," a familiar voice hisses, and the sound is silenced. "Goddamn it. Level four on Wednesday."

Level four?

I try to speak, but my throat won't cooperate. A raspy gasp of air is all I can manage.

"Steve?" My brother takes my hand, and I turn towards his voice, blinking my eyes against the harsh light streaming through the window behind him. "Jesus, mate, you scared the death out of us."

With a frown, I try again to speak. "Wh-what happened?" I croak.

"Here." Brandon hands me a plastic cup of water. He perches on the bed beside me, and it's then I notice the stark white walls surrounding us, and an incessant beeping sound coming from beside me.

"You're in the hospital. There was an accident. You've been in a coma for six months." Tears fill his eyes. "They told us you might not wake up. It was real touch and go there for a minute."

Another siren goes off down the hall, and Brandon lets out a sigh, raking his hand through his hair. "It's an alert from the government." He waves his phone in the air. "We're going into lockdown in two days' time. No leaving our homes for four weeks."

"What?" I ask. "Why would we be locked in our homes for four weeks? Are we at war?" It could be the splitting headache pounding behind my eyes, but nothing is making sense.

"Nah, nothing like that. Well… not really. The world has turned upside down. Never thought I'd see anything like it in my lifetime. It's like we've stepped back in time to when the plague was around. It's a global pandemic. Coronavirus is what they're calling it." He shakes his head. "They say it's like the flu but spreads faster and is more deadly. It's crazy, man."

I frown, my mind not accepting what he's saying. A global pandemic? How is that possible in this day and age?

The last thing I remember is running through the crowded streets and… a flash of something… a car perhaps, then… everything goes a little hazy. Just an endless stream of fuzz.

"I know, right? It only just came to New Zealand, but we've seen how it went down overseas, so Jacinda's locking it down right off the bat. Wherever you are at midnight on Wednesday, that's where you have to stay for four weeks, unless you're an essential worker."

I can't wrap my head around it. One minute I'm running to catch Sarah before her flight, and… Shit. My eyes widen as I turn to my brother. I'm almost afraid to ask. "Did Sarah…?"

Brandon's face drops and he nods. "Yeah, mate. She got on the plane. Sorry."

Tilting my head back, I close my eyes, willing the endless dream to claim me again. To take me away from this alternate universe I seem to have awoken to. Back to when Sarah was with me, and everything made sense. When the only thing that needed to be locked down was your dinner reservation, not your home.

"It's not all bad, mate," Brandon says with a pat of my leg. "Now that you're awake, you get to come hang out with your big brother for four weeks." He grins, but it doesn't reach his eyes. There's something he's not telling me.

"I lost the house, didn't I?"

"Not entirely." His eyes go all squinty, and he fidgets with the bedsheet over my legs.

"Spill."

Letting out a sigh, he rakes his hand through his hair again. "Don't get mad, but the bank was ready to foreclose seeing as you weren't able to make your mortgage payments, so..." He draws out the word, avoiding my gaze.

"So?" I prompt.

"So, I took over the mortgage." He flings his hands out wide. "I'm your new roomie, bro."

Time to Wake was written for an assignment where we had to write about a character waking after a six-month coma. A lot can change in six months, and I imagine it would be quite scary to wake and find things are not as you knew them to be. Throw Corona into the mix and going into lockdowns, and you have yourself a waking nightmare.

Out of my Depth

Still no boats or signs of rescue. My help sign
washed away again last night. I have no energy
to put up a new one.
I'm so hungry. I've been dreaming of a juicy
piece of fish, and I've decided
I have no other options left.
My spear is sharp enough now.
I'm going to try it. Once the sun is high,
and the tide is out, I'm going fishing
in the shark-infested waters.

They're only babies. What harm could they do?

We were given the assignment *Day 52 on a desert island,* and at first I was stumped on how to go about this, but then it hit me. I grabbed a piece of paper, crumpled it up, dabbed tea on it and dripped red nail-polish over it, then wrote this short piece here.

2032

The year is 2032, and haven't we come far?
Petrol prices hiked too high to fuel our flying cars.

We can't remember numbers or how to use a map,
Who needs to know that anyway? It's all found in an app.

Our watches tell us when to sleep or how far we have been
Our lives depend immensely on that of the machines.

No longer can we function using basic common skills,
Instead, we need the internet to pay all of our bills.

Children don't know how to search for facts using a book,
They never learned the struggle of the time it took to look.

The world is at our fingertips, but still we want for more,
Everything's too easy, and life is such a bore.

Yes, the year is 2032, and still we have not learned,
That so much more has meaning when you feel that it is
earned.

2032 was an assignment with the prompt of 2032. I had a lot of fun with this one, picturing a futuristic life based on how things seem to be going in the world today. Covid has certainly changed things up a bit for us, but not as much as the use of technology and machines.

What are Words?

THE CURSOR BLINKS TAUNTINGLY.
No idea.
No idea.
No idea.
It's been four hours of staring at the flickering screen with not an ounce of inspiration. Not one single word or even a lone letter has filled that gap. Only a blank page with that damn blinking cursor; a constant reminder of how far I still have to go.

I shift my gaze to the calendar on the wall with the large red circle around June 12th. I have... I raise my eyes to the ceiling, counting... seven days, five hours, and sixteen minutes to upload my manuscript to the editor, and I'm no closer than I was a month ago.

Fifty thousand words doesn't sound like a lot in the grand scheme of things, not when the first ten thousand flowed out with ease. The remaining forty thousand, however, that's about as daunting as it can get when you're staring at the abyss of writer's block.

Almost six thousand words per day, that's how much I need to write to meet the deadline, but it may as well be a million with the way I'm feeling. Under normal circumstances, I could knock it out in my sleep, but when Mandy walked out three weeks ago, she took my inspiration along with her. My muse, my light, the very reason I put pen to paper in the first place. Without her, the words won't flow. They've dried up like an over-used watering hole in the desert.

My fingers twitch, hovering above the keys I know so well, eager to work. Tentatively, I let them rest in place, the tiny nodules of the F and J keys beneath my index fingers like a beacon welcoming me home. Still the cursor blinks.

No idea.

No idea.

No idea.

Closing my eyes, I tilt my head skyward, searching for divine inspiration. The story is in there somewhere, I know it is. Locked away in the recesses of my mind, waiting for me to find the key. I pick up my phone, swiping the screen until my number one procrastination tool pops open and I begin to scroll. Friends from all over the world dance and chat and mime, occupying my mind and numbing the burning need to finish what I started. When I finally glance up, another half an hour has gone by with no words written.

Pushing my phone aside, I shake out my fingers, twist my head side-to-side, and turn my eyes to the blank screen once more. There's something there. A tiny niggling thought trying to push its way through, and I reach for it, grasping it tightly in my fist before it can run off again. My fingers glide across the keys, one word after another forming before my eyes.

I lean back, breathing a sigh of relief, for this surely can mean only one thing; the dreaded writer's block is no more. I have a sentence. One beautifully eloquent sentence.

The timer goes off, and with a triumphant whoop, I ease the lid of my laptop closed, giving it a loving tap before sliding it into the case. My allotted writing time is up, and though I'm only a fraction closer to my deadline, I can't help but feel a sense of achievement. Today, I did something I've struggled to do in weeks. I got words down.

What are Words was written for a competition with the theme "A hard day's work" and a word limit of 1500. Even though I've worked in factories and retail, there's still nothing quite like staring at a blank page and knowing you've got nothing to add. It can be draining and disheartening, and that's why I chose to write about it. Writing is hard work, and it's made harder by our self-imposed goals and deadlines. Sometimes, you have to take the wins where you can, even if it means only writing one sentence.

Too Good to be True

SARAH PULLED UP OUTSIDE the log cabin nestled in amongst the luscious trees of every shade of green. The nearest town was ten kilometres away, and there were no other houses in sight. She was truly alone. It was almost too good to be true. After the year she'd had, she just wanted some time to herself to regroup and figure out what to do next.

When she'd begun looking into accommodation, most places were out of her budget, but then this little beauty had seemingly fallen into her lap. An ad on Facebook had lured her in with its picturesque charm, and the price had been far less than anything else she'd come across.

She unfurled herself from the car, stretching her arms above her head before retrieving her bag from the back seat and heading inside. The kitchen was quaint; pot belly stove, copper pots hanging above the island in the centre, and a small bay window with planters full of herbs.

The living area was cosy and warm, a roaring fire already burning to take the chill off. She dropped her bag and flopped down on the worn couch, draping herself in the blanket hanging on the back. The drive had been long, and she was exhausted. She'd close her eyes for just a few moments before unpacking and getting properly settled.

Music filled her ears, soft and soothing. She didn't remember switching the radio on, but perhaps it was on a timer. Either way, it was nice. Beethoven maybe? Mozart? She never could tell the difference. The smell of fresh coffee tickled her nostrils. Must be on a timer as well.

She peeled her eyes open, a yawn catching her by surprise. She sat up, twisting her neck side-to-side, and leapt from her seat. "Who are you?" she demanded of the man sitting at the kitchen bench with his hands wrapped around a mug.

"I was going to ask you the same question, but you looked so peaceful, I didn't want to wake you." He smiled, holding his mug up. "Coffee? I just made a pot."

Sarah clutched the blanket to her chest, as if it could shield her from him. "What are you doing here?"

He grabbed another mug and poured the enticing black liquid in. "Sugar? Milk?"

She nodded, waiting him out.

He walked over to the couch, placing her steaming mug on the coffee table. "Here you go." He sat down opposite her. "I'm Mike, and you are?" He held his hand out.

She eyed him warily before accepting his hand. It was rough and calloused. "Sarah," she said.

"You saw the ad on Facebook too, huh?"

Her eyes widened. How could he know that?

He shook his head, chuckling. "I knew there had to be a catch."

"What do you mean?" She frowned.

"The price was ridiculous. I mean, look at this place." He waved his arm around the room, and Sarah took the place in again with fresh eyes. "It was foolish to think anyone would charge so little for it."

He was right. She'd known it when she pulled up, and she knew it now upon further inspection. They'd been set up.

She dropped the blanket to the floor, rubbing a hand down her face. "So you booked to stay here, and so did I," she clarified.

"Looks like it." Mike stretched his arms across the back of the couch. "I hope you don't snore."

Sarah opened her mouth to retort when the sound of gravel crunching beneath tyres caught her attention. She peered out the window behind her to see a cloud of dust moving towards them. She turned back to Mike with wide eyes.

"Guess we're not the only ones who answered the ad," he said, heading back to the kitchen and pouring a coffee for the newcomer.

"Um, I haven't had a chance to look around the place yet," I said. "Just how many rooms are there?"

"Four." He grinned. "Looks like we're having a party."

Too Good to be True was an assignment where we had to write about a bargain vacation with a stranger in a shared cabin. A bit of an odd one, and rather specific, but it was fun. I have added a little onto the end of this one, as our assignments are meant to be 500 words, and I had only just uncovered that they'd both rented the same place at that point. I love the idea of someone secretly renting out rooms to strangers.

Tell me no Lies

"I SWEAR TO GOD, IT'S THE TRUTH!" Joe pulls against his restraints, but it's no use. Even Houdini himself couldn't free himself from the bindings of Virgil St. Clair.

"See, that's not what we heard, was it, boss?" Virgil circles Joe, the toothpick between his teeth flicking side-to-side. "We heard you was in bed with the coppers. Gettin' yourself a nice little pay cheque for informing on some of our acquaintances. Ain't that right, boss?" He sniffs, rubbing his thumb across his nose.

"That's right," comes a voice from the shadows; one that instils fear in men the world over. Marco Demouth is not known for his leniency. He runs a tight ship, and he does not condone deceit of any kind. Especially when it affects his business dealings.

Joe shakes his head. "I didn't do it! I don't even know who Mickey is."

Virgil kicks the legs of the chair out from under him, tipping it backwards. "That's not the way Cassie tells it." He reaches out and drags the blonde woman closer. "You calling her a liar?"

Joe's eyes widen as he glances towards her. He shakes his head vehemently. "No, I would never…"

"Sounds to me like that's exactly what you're doin'," Virgil interrupts. "You're sayin' the boss's daughter didn't tell us it was you?"

"No, I'm not…"

"So you admit it then?"

"No!" Sweat beads on Joe's brow. "I don't deny she told you, or that she heard it, but I'm telling you, it wasn't me. I'm no snitch."

Virgil sucks on the toothpick, shaking his head. "You know how the boss feels about liars, Joe." He drops the woman's arm and stalks into the corner of the room, returning with a can of gasoline.

"W-what are you doing?" Joe fights, struggling against the ropes around his arms and legs. "Please! I swear, it wasn't me!"

Virgil ignores his pleas, unscrewing the cap and tipping the foul-smelling liquid all over Joe's legs, coating his pants. He retrieves a silver lighter from his pocket, flicking the top up and raising a brow. "One last chance."

Tears trail down Joe's cheeks as he begs. "It wasn't me," he whispers, turning his gaze back to Cassie. "Please, tell them…"

"Boss?" Virgil raises a brow in question, but his eyes remain firmly on Joe.

Marco steps out of the shadows, his fingers steepled beneath his chin. "What say you, Cassie? Could you have been mistaken?"

Cassie pulls her lip between her teeth. "I… I don't…" She swallows, taking a step back.

"You don't what, sweetheart?"

Virgil spins the wheel on the lighter, igniting the wick. "Tick, tock."

"Please!" Joe cries out, and the scent of urine permeates the air. "I have a wife and kids at home. Don't do this."

"Cassie?" Marco watches his daughter as she wrings her hands together. "You wouldn't lie to me, would you?"

Her face crumples. "I'm s-sorry," she whispers, burying her face in her hands. "It wasn't him."

The lighter clicks closed, and Joe heaves a sigh of relief, his head falling to his chest.

"You disappoint me." Marco nods at Virgil, and he takes up the can of gasoline. "You leave me no choice." He turns on his heels, leaving the room as the flint catches and her screams ring through the air.

Tell me no Lies was an assignment titled "Liar, liar, pants on fire." As you can see, I took it quite literally! A little darker than my norm, but it's actually one of my favourites. I wanted to explore the idea of how far a father would go to protect his business, even if it meant the destruction of his family, while also playing on the old rhyme and having the liar's pants literally go up in flames.

The Roles we Play

MOST OF THEM ARE BLURRED, but a few of the images I managed to salvage from the roll hold me captive. I can't quite believe what I'm seeing. Crowds of people watching a processional down Colombo Street, and there in the foreground, looking directly at the camera, is my brother, his face partially covered by his cap.

"Soooo," Poppy draws out the word, her mouth pulled into a grimace. "What do you think this means?"

"I think it's apparent, isn't it?"

"Is it though? I mean, you can't *really* make out a lot." She squints as if she can't see the glaringly obvious. She can't be so dense as to not have figured it out.

"Look." I point out the familiar open top Rolls Royce driving down the centre of the road in the first shot. There's a man standing in the back, his hand held high in a wave. Beside him is a woman with a large red hat and lace covering her face. Even from this angle it's obvious it's the Prime Minister and First Lady.

"Okay, yeah, but we don't know it's from *that* day though, do we? And he's just standing there."

I shake my head, scrolling to the next image. He's standing back from the crowd, hidden by a cluster of trees. His hand is shoved deep into his pocket.

Poppy reaches out and stays my hand. "Maybe we should stop. We don't need to see any more."

Only I've already seen them. I just needed Poppy to see it too, to make sure my mind isn't playing tricks on me.

I scroll on.

His arm is outstretched, aiming at the vehicle as it passes by.

I click again.

People are running. A lone woman in a trench coat walks away with her head ducked down, and my brother is nowhere to be seen.

Poppy doesn't say anything as she stares at the incriminating image, her shaking hand held to her lips.

I click a button and the screen goes blank, just the shining light of the projector on the white wall.

"What are you going to do?" she whispers, her face now as white as the wall before us.

"I'm handing it in."

"But they'll lock him up. For good."

"I know, and as much as I hate the idea of him being locked up, I have to do this. I can't stand the thought of an innocent man rotting away in prison for the rest of his life, knowing what I do." I turn pleading eyes to her, begging her to understand.

"I can't let you do this."

"Poppy, I know you love him, but we can't just wish it away. Jason did this. He's guilty." I place my hand on her forearm, but she swats me away.

"He was following orders." She pulls her trench coat on and tugs the roll of film from the projector. "And you'd be wise to follow them too."

The Roles we Play was written for an assignment with the prompt; *you find a roll of film; how does the story pan out?* It took me right up until the day it was due to come up with something, and I had to rewrite the ending several times before I was happy with it. This one, as you can probably guess, is inspired by the JFK shooting.

Stunned Mullet

"WHAT'LL IT BE, DOLL?" The perky blonde chews her gum loudly as she fastens a cape around my neck.

My fingers twitch, reaching for the silk scarf I'd tied around my head before walking out the door. The same one I'd been wearing the past week.

I meet her eyes in the mirror, and she gives me an encouraging smile. Huffing out a sigh, I slowly tug the scarf free, letting it fall to the floor, and behind me, the hairdresser stifles a gasp.

It's bad. I know it is.

Swallowing the lump in my throat, I raise my mournful eyes to hers. "Can you fix it? Please tell me you can fix it."

She clicks her tongue, her nimble fingers tugging at the short tufts on top and the longer sections at the back.

I don't know what came over me. It had seemed like such a good idea at the time; God only knows why.

I'd been scrolling reel after reel of people giving themselves cute dos and they made it look so easy. Something even I, the girl who has not a creative bone in her body, could manage. Alas, my scissors had other ideas.

After the first snip, I knew I'd made a mistake and tried to rectify it by cutting the other side to even it up. It only made things worse. Again and again I tried, snipping one piece here and another there, trying desperately to fix my error, but it was too late. Before I knew it, I was sitting on the floor, surrounded by the massacre of my once gorgeous locks, tears streaming down my face as I gulped back a wine and stared at what appeared to be something akin to the 'business in the front, party in the back' style of the 80s. Only, my business looked more like it'd been attacked by a lawnmower.

That was a week ago, and I hadn't stepped foot out the door since.

"Well?" I peer up at her with hopeful eyes. "Is it salvageable?"

She grins, taking hold of my shoulders. "Of course, hon. This ain't my first lockdown lop off."

I'd been struggling to write after a year of pushing myself to release a record number of books, and for whatever reason, this assignment (Bad hair day) was the first thing I'd written and felt good about in months.

There are photos of me as a youngster with a hideous haircut, much like the one I described, though it was intentional back then. It was the 80s and acceptable then! But that, along with the memory of me cutting my hair short during lockdown, was what I based this story on. Luckily, my DIY haircut didn't turn out as bad as the poor woman in my story!

A Moment in Time

Sticky sap oozes over hard, knotted wood
Leaves gently whisper on the breeze.
Birds sing a chorus from high up yonder
As they build their nests with ease.

Down below, in the shade, I rest my weary head
Staring up at the dappled sky of blue
All around the world continues turning,
But I am stuck on thoughts of you.

The way your laugh would make me smile,
The twinkle in your eyes so bright.
The way your arms could bring such comfort
On a cold and lonely night.

You were my rock, my saving grace,
My anchor in choppy ocean waves.
You guided me and kept me sane,
Even through some close shaves.

Beneath our tree, I sit and wonder
As tears slide down my cheek,
If I could've changed our ending,
If only I weren't so weak.

A single breath, a moment in time
Was all it took to lose
The one who meant the world to me,
The one I'd always choose.

In the shade of our tree, with closed eyes, I lay,
No more dappled sky of blue do I see,
No more songs from birds up high,
Just thoughts of you and me.

This one came out of nowhere. I was going through my assignments and instant writing exercises, and came across one where we had to describe being a character up in a tree, and for some reason, that stood out to me. I took the parts I liked most and wrote them into the first paragraph of this poem, and then the rest kind of flowed from there.

Atlantis

*Through the veil of the sea, the city of Atlantis waits for
me.*
*She holds her secrets to her chest, her treasures hidden
beneath the depths.*

DEEP GREEN WAVES crashed against the hull of The
Rose, rocking it gently as it journeyed across the large
stretch of water. With the sun just kissing the horizon,
the ocean had an almost ethereal glow. Ahead, a jagged
rock face jutted out from the middle of nowhere, and
Cezarne Peters could just make out the tiny cluster of
islands to its left. Lowering her looking glass, she
nodded to Bilkins. "I see it." The first point to the
triangle.

Dartanian Foxworthy turned his ruddy face to her
with a toothy grin. "Told you I'd find it." His fingers
curled around the rail of the bow, pulling at the
bindings on his wrist. It didn't seem to bother him as he
leaned forward, turning his face skyward.

"Your cockiness is unbecoming, boy."

The taunt hit its mark, and Dartanian stepped his
bulky frame away from the railing. He puffed out his
chest. "I ain't no boy."

Cezarne canted her head, letting her eyes roam
freely over his muscular torso and stubbled jaw. She

was well aware he was no boy. No, Dartanian Foxworthy was *all* man. It was a pity she had to keep him tied up.

"I'm well aware." She let her eyes take one last stroll along his chiselled form before nodding across the ocean. "You've done well to show me this, but I need the others if I'm to find the Lost City of Atlantis."

He quirked a brow, widening his stance against the rocking of the ship. "The Lost City? But no one has come close to finding it."

Trailing a finger along Dartanian's jaw, Cezarne clicked her tongue. "That's why they call it The *Lost* City." She palmed his cheek. "And you're going to lead me there."

"But I don't know where it is!"

"Ah, but that's where you're wrong, Mr. Foxworthy. I happen to know you were aboard the ship Bermuda before she went down." She knew this because she too was meant to be aboard. In fact, she was meant to captain the ship, only to be thwarted by the man before her. She let her hand slide from his face to his chest, pressing herself against him. "And I know what her destination was."

His eyes widened as he stumbled back, an incredulous laugh falling from his lips. "You're mad, you are. She never made it to her destination, did she? So how the bleedin' heck would I know where it is?"

Cezarne pointed her finger into his chest. "Because, as the lone survivor, you know where she went down. And you're going to take me there."

He reared back as if she'd slapped him, his gaze seeking out Bilkins. "She's lost her damn mind, mate."

Without a blink of the eye, Bilkins was in front of Dartanian, his blade pressed to the soft flesh of his throat. "That's our captain you're talking about. You best show some respect."

Dartanian swallowed thickly and nodded. "Yes, sir."

Bilkins held the knife firm, allowing a trickle of blood to lazily drip down Dartanian's neck before he stepped back. He wiped the blade on a kerchief and shoved it back into its scabbard.

"Now that that's settled." Cezarne took her place behind the wheel, spinning it counterclockwise. The ship sliced through the water towards the islands. "Where do we go from here?"

Dartanian hesitated briefly before stumbling back to the bow. His head swivelled this way and that, his lips moving in silent conversation with himself. "That way." He raised his bound hands and pointed northwest, around the island cluster and rock face.

"Very well then." She adjusted the wheel.

"No, I meant *around* the islands." Dartanian turned to her with a frown. "You're headed right for them."

She smiled. "Exactly."

Closing his eyes, he made the sign of the cross with his hands.

"Have a little faith, Mr. Foxworthy." She cackled, turning her attention to the crow's nest above. "What see you, Bones?"

A scraggly haired man poked his head over the side. "Just them there rocks and islands, Cap'n." He pointed a long finger. "Naught else but sea."

Cezarne nodded. "Keep watching. We'll lose light soon, and I don't want any surprises."

"Aye, aye, Cap'n." He cleared his throat before hollering, "And them rocks, Cap'n?"

"What of them?"

"Beggin' your pardon, Cap'n, but we're lookin' ta hit 'em."

Cezarne pulled her looking glass from her pocket and raised it to her eye. "So we are." She smirked, holding her hands firm on the wheel. If this was going to work, she needed to keep true.

The sun had all but disappeared now, and in its place was a sliver of a moon. Barely a glint of light was cast across the ocean waves, allowing them to see very little. Cezarne drew on her other senses. The feel of The Rose beneath her feet, the smell of salty air whipping her hair, the sound of waves crashing in the distance. The rocks were fast approaching.

"Cap'n?" Bones called once more, his voice unsteady.

"Not yet." Cezarne braced herself. Stories told of tumultuous waves surrounding the triangle, and this cluster of islands being the first point, she was expecting the worst. Many a captain had tried but failed to sail across the triangle, present company included, but Cezarne was not about to be another statistic.

The Rose creaked as the waves grew in size and ferocity. Cezarne shifted her feet, her eyes zeroed in on the blackness in front of them. Dartanian had lowered himself to the deck, his head on his knees as he mumbled prayers to whatever God would listen.

"Cap'n?" Bones cried out, worry and confusion colouring his tone.

Bilkins rushed to the bow, leaning as far over the rails as possible. "Almost!" He held his hand out behind him, palm down, as he watched. "Almost!"

Cezarne waited with bated breath for the signal.

"Now!" Bilkins called as he flipped his hand up.

Cezarne spun the wheel hard right, and the ship groaned as it fought the waves. There was a grinding from below as the keel connected with land, but not enough to bring them to a halt. The Rose narrowly missed the jutting rocks as she turned eastward.

At the helm, Cezarne watched the rocks until they were at their backs before spinning the wheel back the other way. The first hurdle was complete.

Bilkins bellowed, pumping a fist in the air. "We made it!"

Cezarne couldn't help but smile, though she knew they still had a way to go. For the past five years, Cezarne had pored over maps and coordinates, marking out each sunken ship and their trajectories. Everything pointed to this one area, and now that she had confirmation of the Bermuda's whereabouts, she knew she was on the right track.

Now, past the point of no return, The Rose sailed on smooth seas beneath an eerily quiet sky. Even the ship herself had ceased her creaks and moans as she rocked Dartanian to sleep in her arms. Bilkins and Bones had taken their leave, getting what rest they could before the true test ahead of them. The veil.

As dawn broke several hours later, The Rose picked up speed, gliding through the cresting waves with ease. In the crow's nest, Bones held his looking glass aloft, scanning their surrounds. "There!" he called down the mast, his eyes bright with excitement.

Cezarne followed his pointing finger, bringing her own looking glass to her eye. A slow smile curled her lips. "You beautiful man, Bones! You've found it!" She adjusted the wheel, correcting their course.

Dartanian stared across the ocean, a frown marring his face. "*That* is The Lost City?" He shook his head. "You're even crazier than I thought if you think two stone pillars is a city." He shot a furtive glance towards Bilkins.

"Ye of little faith." Cezarne smirked. Of course the stone pillars weren't The Lost City. They were just the doorway. "Bilkins, hoist the mainsail."

"Aye, aye, Captain."

A flurry of wind caught the sail and The Rose lurched forward, her hull creating waves of her own. The carved mermaid on the bowsprit pointed towards their target; the centre of the two pillars.

"What are you… You can't be meaning to go between them?" Dartanian marched towards her with an air of rebellion. "You're mad. She'll never make it."

"I am, and she will." Cezarne narrowed her eyes on the man before her. She'd never known him to be a coward. "You're quite welcome to go below deck if you're scared, Mr. Foxworthy. Hell, you can jump overboard if you're that worried. I have no use of you now." She waved him away, knowing full well he'd never jump. Dartanian Foxworthy was the only captain of the seven seas she knew to be averse to swimming.

"Ah, Cap'n?" Bones hung his head over the side, peering down at her. "Me eyes are fixin' ta show me somethin' funny." He glanced ahead then back to her. "Is the air… Is it a wobblin'?"

"Never to mind, Bones. All is well." She grinned, surging full steam ahead.

"Would you look at that?" Bilkins came to stand beside her, a mischievous glint in his eyes. "You were bloody right, Captain." He slapped a hand to her shoulder before hooting out a laugh. "Right where you said an' all."

Sweeping her hand out to her side, Cezarne took a bow. "Of course I was, Bilkins. Did you ever doubt me?"

"Not a once." He stared out at the shimmering air hanging between the pillars. "Not a once."

"What is that?" Dartanian asked, his mouth agape. He stumbled to the bow, hanging onto the railing as he squinted his eyes. "A mirage?"

"It's the veil."

"The veil?"

"*Through the veil of the sea…*"

"—the city of Atlantis waits for me," he finished for her, his eyes wide.

"Precisely."

The stone pillars with crumbling edges loomed ever closer, the gap between them seeming to narrow farther. *This is it,* she thought, bracing herself for impact.

Dartanian dropped to his knees, his hands still holding firm to the railings as he peered through the gaps. Bilkins stood beside him, facing the veil head on.

Above, Bones had swung his legs over the crow's nest and shimmied down the mizzenmast to land beside Cezarne with a thud.

"Hold on!" she cried, wrenching the wheel side-to-side.

The Rose smashed against one then the other pillar, and the air filled with the sound of splintering wood as the ship began to take on water.

"She's not gonna make it!" Bones cried, and for a brief moment, Cezarne wondered if she'd made a mistake. But then the glittering veil before them wrapped itself around The Rose like a cloak, enveloping them in its embrace. The pillars disappeared, and the sky turned a deep purple, then black, as if night had fallen early.

Silence, but for the shuffling of Dartanian's feet. "Are we dead?" he asked.

"Of course not," Bilkins said gruffly. "Right?"

"I don't think so." Cezarne walked in a circle around the wheel. She could hear nothing. No water rushing in, no waves crashing. Nothing. Perhaps they *had* died, for as far as she was aware, ships could not mend themselves.

Unsure of their fate or even how to navigate without the stars to guide her, Cezarne let The Rose lead the way. After a few minutes, a tiny beacon of light took shape, growing until they could see lush green lands.

Blinking away the dark, Cezarne took in her surroundings. It was like nothing she'd ever seen before, and yet familiar all at the same time. Stone pillars with deep green vines clinging to them stuck up from the ground, and large leafy trees hung across the river they now appeared to be gliding down. The iridescent sky above was coloured in shades of pink, blue, and green.

The Rose followed the river around a curve where trees laden with golden fruit lined the edges, and beyond them, a large stone statue of a man dressed in robes towered.

"I don't believe it," Dartanian said in awe. "We're really here." He pointed at the statue. "I've seen his likeness before."

"His name is Atlas, son of Poseidon, and he was the ruler of these lands." Cezarne turned to Bones. "Lower the anchor. I should like to look around."

While he scurried off, she continued. "Some say he built a temple of gold in honour of his father. One so large it's said to reach the clouds above." She tilted her head back, taking in the beatific colours streaking the sky. "A tribute fitting for the creator of this oasis."

The clanking of the anchor ruptured the silence, giving them pause. Birds took flight, darting across the river and up into the skies. The Rose lurched to a stop, and Bilkins pushed the gangplank out to rest along the shore. With Cezarne in the lead, they each walked across the plank and to the land.

"This way," she said, traipsing through thick foliage towards the statue. If her readings had been correct, what she sought would be at his feet.

"How do you know where you're going?" Dartanian asked as he swiped branches away from his face with a huff. "Anyone would think you'd been here before."

"Ah." Cezarne touched her finger to the side of her nose. "That would be telling now, wouldn't it, Mr. Foxworthy?"

He turned to Bones with a thumb hooked in Cezarne's direction. "Does she always talk in riddles like this?"

"Aye, she does." He sniggered. "Tis what ya like 'bout her."

Dodging a swinging vine, Dartanian scoffed. "I don't think so."

Bones guffawed, shaking his head. "Righto then." He marched ahead, using his cutlass to carve a path.

"There he is," Bilkins said in reverence as he stared up at the behemoth statue. "The mighty Atlas."

"A fine specimen if ever I saw one." Cezarne winked, barrelling ahead to the plinth he rested on. She climbed atop a ridge running around the bottom edge and peered between the statue's legs. "A sight to behold." She turned to Bilkins with a grin. "It's here."

"Bring him," Bilkins called back to Bones, who in turn nudged Dartanian forward.

"A right treat an' all, init?" He gestured for Dartanian to join their captain on the plinth. With a confused look over his shoulder, he obliged. Cezarne had her hands in a large bowl of water resting between Atlas's feet.

"What's all this then?"

Cezarne held her cupped hands out to him. "Drink."

Dartanian scrunched his nose. "I don't think so."

Her brows lowered, and she scowled at him. "Drink," she said again, forcefully.

Huffing out a sigh, Dartanian leaned his head forward, wrapping his lips around the tips of her fingers, and suckled the water until it was gone. Cezarne's eyes searched his, waiting.

"How do you feel?"

He blinked once, twice, three times. "I feel…" His eyes darted about, as if seeing their surrounds for the first time. "Where are we?" His voice was quiet, filled with awe, until he looked down to see his hands were tied. Raising them to her, he asked, "Why are my hands bound? What's going on?"

Cezarne grinned, reaching her hand to palm his cheek. "We found it," she whispered, glancing up at the statue.

Dartanian followed her gaze, stumbling back and falling to the ground. "Is that…?" Cezarne nodded. "And this is…?"

She nodded again. "Atlantis."

His eyes widened, his mouth opening and closing. "We found it," he whispered. Then, shaking his head, he frowned. "But, how? The last thing I remember was the Bermuda." He winced, his cheeks flaming. "Sorry about that, by the way."

Cezarne shook her head dismissively. "Water under the bridge. Continue."

He turned his gaze skyward. "The Bermuda was hit by a storm out of nowhere, and she went down. And then…" He shook his head.

"Go on."

"You'll think me foolish."

"Try me."

He closed his eyes, sucking in a breath. "I remember seeing a… a mermaid, or at least something that looked like a mermaid, with long flowing hair and a tail. She carried me to safety."

Cezarne nodded. When he'd been found washed ashore with no recollection of who he was, she'd had her suspicions. Lore spoke of mermaids granting safety to those found in the sea but, as with all mystical creatures, their help does not come for free. The price; your memories.

"What you speak is true, my love. That's why I had to find the elixir of Atlas." She smiled, caressing his cheek. "I couldn't have you forgetting me."

He grasped her hand. "I could never forget you."

Bones snorted. "Told ya. Them riddles is what ya like." He clapped his hand to Dartanian's shoulder. "Good ta 'ave ya back, sir."

"Bones, Bilkins." Dartanian pushed up from the ground, only now noticing his fellow shipmates. He held his hands, still bound, out to them both. Bones took hold, shaking them both, but Bilkins turned his nose up, huffing sullenly.

"You're still sore about the Bermuda, I take it, Bilkins? I *am* sorry."

"And well you should be too. We're a team, we are. You deserted us." He pointed a finger at Dartanian's chest. "And you hurt the captain." He jutted his chin, and Dartanian nodded his agreement.

"That I did, and I promise to make up for it however she sees fit." He turned his attention back to the blonde-haired beauty. "Can you ever forgive me?"

Tapping a finger to her chin, she walked in a slow circle. "Hmmm, let me think. I suppose you *did* help me find what I've spent my life looking for." She grinned, wrapping her arms around his neck and planting a kiss upon his lips. "It's only fair."

Atlantis was an entry for the Sunday Star Times short story competition. There was no theme to follow, only a 3000-word limit. I wrote 2999!

A little fun fact for you
When I was a teenager, I worked at the local library, and there was a member there with the name Cezarne. I'd never seen any name more beautiful before, and it stuck with me. It seemed only fitting to be the name of my buccaneering captain.

Autumn Daze

Pink cheeks, cold nose,
Breath puffing out like mist.
Hands tucked in pockets,
Fingers in a fist.

Beanie pulled down over ears,
Scarf around the neck.
Thick socks, warm boots;
Everything in check.

Leaves of orange and of red,
Crunching beneath feet.
Trees no longer dressed in green;
Their clothes spread like a sheet.

Hews of gold and amber,
The sky darkens to grey.
Quickened steps, down the path,
On this chilly autumn day.

Up ahead a library glows
With warm lights through the pane,
And scattered all about the place
Are books to feed the brain.

Scarf and hat discarded,
Curled upon a corner chair,
Descending into fantasy;
A land so far from here.

Escape the chill of autumn breeze
Inside a book of spring,
Where flowers bloom, the sky is blue,
And birds begin to sing.

While outside it gets colder,
The sun no longer high,
A world between the pages
Makes the time go by.

And when the journey's over,
The last page turned to close,
Scarf and hat are donned again,
Cool air tickling the nose.

Head tucked against the wind,
Back down the path once more,
Through the gate and up the steps,
Rushing through the door.

Home sweet home, or so they say,
Though I have to disagree.
The library with all its books
Is where I'd rather be.

Unlike most of the stories and poems in this collection, this one didn't come from an assignment or competition prompt. I had been struggling to write for some time, and so I asked my daughter to give me a prompt. As soon as she suggested 'autumn', I instantly pictured leaves crunching and curling up with a book, thus *Autumn Daze* was born.

$\mathcal{R}espect$

"SO, WHAT DO YOU THINK?" Joe leans back in his seat, his legs spread wide and one arm dangling between them.

"What do I think?" I stare at him, not quite sure how to form a coherent sentence to respond.

"Yeah. I mean, like I said…" He sits forward, swiping his thumb across his nose. "It's going to benefit both of us. You especially." The crooked grin he gives me would've melted my insides once upon a time. Now all it does is make me want to punch him in his stupid face.

I run my tongue along my front teeth, closing my eyes and inhaling deeply to keep myself from acting on my impulses. What he's suggesting is the most arrogant, misogynistic idea I've ever heard, and he's staring at me as if he's a genius doing me a huge favour. And sure, to his mates, he probably would seem that way if I were to go along with this cockamamie bullshit, but thanks to my Aretha Franklin phase in my adolescence, I have more self-respect than that.

"As tempting as the offer is, I'm gonna have to say no."

He frowns, taking hold of my hands. "Babe, come on. Think about it. You get all of this—" he runs a hand down his torso as if he's some sort of delectable treat,

"—with none of the pressure to perform for me in the bedroom every night."

"Oh gee, when you put it that way…"

His lips curl into a slow grin. "I knew you'd agree."

"…It's still a hard no from me." Dragging my hand out of his grasp, I stand, hooking my bag over my shoulder. "I'll grab my things in the morning." With my head held high, I march for the door without so much as a second glance. Even his big brown puppy-dog eyes won't stop me from walking out.

"Babe," he calls, but I ignore him, waving my hand over my shoulder. I'm not his babe anymore, and if I'm honest, I haven't been for months. What could have been a beautiful relationship changed swiftly the second I moved into his cramped one-bedroom apartment. All of a sudden I went from being the sexy girlfriend to the live-in surrogate mother, taking care of all the cooking and cleaning while also holding down a full time job. He'd come home and sprawl on the couch, gaming or scrolling through his phone, oblivious to me cleaning around him, and never lifting his finger unless it was to push a button on the remote.

And he has the audacity to suggest an open relationship where he gets his end away elsewhere, while I sit at home waiting for him like a good little girlfriend, and say it's for *my* benefit. I don't think so.

I should've run for the hills the moment I saw his overflowing sink and laundry hamper, but like a lovesick puppy, I ignored the signs. It's funny what a few months can do for your perspective.

From now on, I'm flying solo. I'm going my own way. I'm—

"Oof." My face explodes in pain, my phone clatters to the floor, as does my bag, and I stumble backwards. Two firm hands grab hold of my arms, catching me before I lose my balance completely.

"Shit, are you okay?" Four of the brightest blue eyes stare back at me, and all thoughts of being a strong, independent woman fly out the window never to be seen again.

I blink up at him, my nose and forehead throbbing.

He waves his hand in front of my face. "How many fingers am I holding up?"

"Uh, three?" I manage, though I don't sound convincing to my own ears. Bright spots dance before my eyes, but I'm almost positive of my answer.

"Phew. You had me worried there. I know I can be a Neanderthal, but I didn't think my head was that dense to give you a concussion." He rubs his hand against the back of his head.

It takes me a minute to connect the dots between my throbbing face and his Neanderthal head, but when it finally clicks, I'm sure my face turns a lovely shade of crimson. "Oh my… shit, are *you* okay?" I reach for his shoulders, spinning him around so I can examine the back of his head.

He chuckles, and the sound vibrates through my hands. "I'm fine. Should've been looking where I was going."

"I ran into you. I think it's me who should've been paying attention. I'm so sorry."

"Honestly, I'm fine." He stoops down, picking up my phone and handing it to me. His lips pull into a thin line as he tentatively runs a finger along my forehead, eliciting a hiss from me. "Are you sure *you're* okay? That's quite the bump."

"To be honest, I'm more embarrassed than hurt. I can't believe I ran into you like that. I'm such a klutz." A klutz with a pounding head.

He shrugs. "Accidents happen. And you obviously had a lot on your mind." He glances behind me. "You're up in 5A, right? With Joe?"

"I was, yeah." I offer him a sheepish smile. "You could say I just handed in my notice."

His eyebrows lift, and he tucks his hands in his pockets. "That's unfortunate for Joe."

I roll my eyes, then wince at the sharp jolt of pain that follows. "Believe me, he won't be pining over me. In fact, I'd be surprised if he doesn't have someone in the wings already waiting after the conversation we just had."

He sucks a breath in through his teeth. "Sounds like you're better off without him."

I pull myself up taller, nodding. "I am. I can't be what he needs me to be, and he's definitely not what I need or want."

"Well, uh…" He chuckles. "Sorry, I don't even know your name."

"Candace."

"Well, Candace, it's his loss. For what it's worth, I think he's an idiot."

A laugh bubbles up and out. "You don't even know me."

"I like to think of myself as a pretty good judge of character, and you, Candace, seem like a genuinely nice person. One I wouldn't mind getting to know better. It's a pity we met under such circumstances." He offers a smile and holds out his hand. "I'm Mark, by the way."

His hand is warm, his shake firm, solid, and when he smiles, his eyes light up. "Mark." The word rolls off my tongue like a caress, and I gently slide my hand from his. "Maybe I'll see you around sometime." Grabbing my bag from the floor, I give him a nod as I step around him. "It was nice bumping into you."

This one was inspired by conversations with friends, and the song "Flowers" by Miley Cyrus. So many times we read stories of women who are pushovers or too shy for their own good, and I wanted to have a strong character who knows her worth.

A Date with Disaster

"OF COURSE, YOU KNOW, he's one of those lizard people, so you've gotta—"

"I'm gonna stop you right there," I say, holding my palm up. "Um, what? Lizard people?"

Stuart leans back in his seat with a smarmy smirk on his face that just makes me want to punch him. "You don't know about the lizard people?"

"Uh, no, can't say that I do." But I'm sure I'm about to find out.

He runs his tongue along his top teeth as he glances around the room before shuffling his seat forward and piercing me with an almost deranged stare. "Buckle in, baby. I'm about to blow your mind."

I wish someone would blow my mind right now. Blow it right out of this dinky restaurant, if it can even be called that, and straight back to my sofa with a drink of Jamesons and a slice of pizza. At least I could flick through Netflix to keep entertained instead of listening to whatever conspiracy theory this guy is on about. I should've known it was going to be an epic fail the moment I saw his screen name; BigDaddy69. Only a douchebag would come up with that. Or someone overcompensating for something. Either way, there most definitely will not be a second date. Hell, I can barely stay awake for the one I'm currently in.

"…and that's why you know old Bill has gotta be one of them, because he's planting shit in our brains…"

Oh Jesus, this one is off the rails. What the hell did I get myself into?

"…haven't you ever noticed how the ads are customised to suit you?" He taps his forehead. "They're always listening, watching, learning." He leans back again, folding his arms. "Subliminal messages, man."

"Right." I draw out the word as I signal to the waiter. I'm going to need a lot more alcohol to deal with this maniac. "So, when I go on the book of faces and see an ad for a unicorn onesie, that's the lizard people brainwashing me, is it?"

Stuart nods, his eyes glinting as if I've somehow agreed with the horseshit streaming from his mouth.

"And what exactly is that going to achieve? If I buy said onesie?"

"It's all about compliance. They plant seeds inside your brain and make you think it was your idea. They're building up to something bigger." He holds his hands up, a metre apart. "And old Bill's not the only one, either." He waggles his brows, bracing his hands on the table. "I heard they've infiltrated all the major governments around the globe, including here. That's how they'll eventually take over."

"Let me get this straight, you think Cindy is a lizard in disguise?"

"Oh no." He shakes his head. "Not her. But the opposition…" He widens his eyes and nods. "She most definitely is. In fact, I wouldn't be surprised if the whole party is in on it."

"The whole of the National party are lizards trying to take over the country?"

He drums his fingers on the table. "Exactly."

Jesus, Mary, and Joseph. I watch him take a swig of his drink, swiping the back of his hand across his wet lips with a grin, and I can't help but wonder exactly how much of the Kool-Aid this guy has been drinking. He's probably one of those guys who thinks there was no moon landing either, or that Elvis is still alive and kicking.

"Can I ask you something?" He looks at me expectantly, so I nod. It can't be any worse than the current topic of conversation. "What do you really think they're hiding in Area 51?"

I stand corrected.

"Because I think it's the hibernation tank for the lizard people. You know, where they implant their lizard foetuses into fertile human women."

My eyes widen as I inadvertently suck in a breath while at the same time taking a sip of my drink. A cough erupts from deep in my chest, and I fight to place the glass down on the table while my body convulses, trying to rid my lungs of the Jamesons and ginger ale they have inhaled.

"Are you alright?" he asks, glancing sidewards, as if *I'm* the embarrassing one.

"I'm fine," I choke out, thumping a hand into my chest. A waitress stops by the table, offering a glass of water, and I accept with a forced smile. "I'm good." I drag in another shaky breath, my eyes wet with the unshed tears that form when your life flashes before your eyes. I thump another hand to my chest, letting out another barking cough.

Stuart frowns at me, his lips pulled to the side as if he's trying to work me out. His eyes seem to dart about my face, and his lips quiver as he speaks to himself under his breath. Then his eyes widen, and he pushes back from the table, a finger pointed in my direction. "I know what you are!"

"Excuse me?" I dab a napkin beneath my eyes.

"You're one of them," he hisses.

I sigh, leaning my elbows on the table. "One of who?"

"The lizard people!" He doesn't even try to hide the idiocy coming from his mouth. "I'm right, aren't I? That's why you reacted that way. Area 51 is where it's all happening." He shakes his head, muttering to himself.

Is it too much to ask that I find a decent guy and *not* one who probably lives in his parents' basement making hats out of tinfoil? Because I know that's what this guy is normally doing on a Friday night. I'm probably the only person desperate enough to have swiped right on him. I won't make that mistake again.

I'm ready to call it a night. I gave it my best shot, but this date needs to end, now. There's only one way to do this. I raise my bare wrist to my lips, whispering, "He's onto me. He knows too much."

His eyes flick up to me, widening, and he swallows audibly. "Wh-who are you talking to? Who is that?" he demands, pointing at my arm.

I glance up at him and nod. "Roger that. Protocol Alpha?"

His face turns white and a sheen of perspiration hangs on his top lip. "P-protocol Alpha?"

I turn my body to the side. "Elimination? Are you sure?" I make a point of peering over my shoulder at him. "If you say so." Pressing my thumb to my wrist, I clear my throat and stand, tugging at the hem of my top before swivelling to face the now empty table and the retreating back of Stuart. With a chuckle, I sit back down and grab my glass, downing it in one. Raising my hand, I signal to the waitress. "Can you have our meals boxed up to go please? Change of plans." I plaster on a smile.

She eyes the vacant seat opposite me. "Both of them?"

"Sure, why the hell not? May as well get something good out of this date."

Her brows arch and she nods with a knowing smile. "We've all been there."

I laugh, crunching on an ice cube. "I very much doubt it."

I was listening to a podcast a while back, and they were talking about conspiracy theories. I was so captivated by the crazy stories they believed, and it made me think how that would play out in a dating situation. I wasn't sure where I was going to go with it, and I had toyed with the idea of turning it into something full length, but so far, it hasn't gone any further. I did use it for an assignment about a first date though.

Who is Santa?

Tis the eve of Christmas, a day full of glee,
When children awake to gifts under the tree.

I ready the reindeer and check over the sleigh,
It's nearing the time when we must be away.

The elves are still building, their fingers so nimble,
Painting a scene on the head of a thimble.

When out of the workshop, a scooter rolls free,
And without any warning, it flies into me.

I land with a thud on the snow-covered ground,
My head hits the sleigh, and it's starting to pound.

My eyes flutter closed as darkness unfolds,
But I'm shaken awake by someone in gold.

"You have to get up," he says with a frown.
"Now's not the time to be lying down.

"Children are sleeping and counting on you.
You have to get up, there's so much to do."

I climb to my feet with my head in my hands,

And that's when I realise, I know not of these lands.

"Where am I?" I ask. "And what do you mean?"
This place is not like any other I've seen.

"You're Santa," he says. "Good ol' Saint Nick.
And you need to get moving, quicker than quick."

He points to the reindeer then to a sleigh.
"It's time to get in. You must be on your way."

"You must be confused. I can't be Saint Nick.
I'm just a man, and I have no magic."

Clicking my fingers to show that he's wrong,
I'm shocked when the sleigh starts to belt a familiar
song.

"You are him," he says, "and there's no time to dally.
Your first stop is Dallas, and her name is Sally."

He gives me a push and encouraging smile.
The guy is quite clearly stuck in denial.

"I don't even know how to get there," I say.
"Just climb in," he says. "They know the way."

He points to the reindeer that stamp at the snow,
And for whatever reason, I cannot say no.

I climb into the sleigh all loaded with toys,
To deliver to all of the girls and the boys.

I tug on the reins but don't get very far.
At this point it's probably faster by car.

A memory unfurls of stories we told,
And deep in my mind, it starts to unfold…

"On Holly, on Jolly, on Folly," I try.
But they don't move a muscle, no blink of the eye.

"On Cherry, and Mary, on Jerry and Ben.
On Gertie, and Mertyl, and is one of them Glen?"

Still nothing happens, no reindeer take flight.
How will we do this in only one night?

I squeeze my eyes shut and try to remember,
The stories and songs we heard every December.

Something unravels and starts to take shape.
I open my eyes, my mouth all agape.

"On Dasher, and Dancer, on Prancer, and Vixen.
On Comet, and Cupid, on Donner, and Blitzen."

Then all of a sudden, we're up in the air,
And down below us the elves start to cheer.

We dip and we dive through a flutter of snow
And out of my mouth bursts a "Ho, Ho, Ho, Ho!"

Every year we have a Christmas get together, and we usually have to write a Christmas poem. This time they decided to make it easier on those who aren't fond of poetry and gave us the option to write a story or poem using the words Holly, Jolly, and Folly.

It took me a while to come up with a way to use those words, but then it came to me while watching *The Santa Clause* one night. A Santa who has forgotten he's Santa and has to remember who he is and how he does what he does.

Tea for Two

"YOU'RE A LIFESAVER, JODI. Our last babysitter did a disappearing act on us." Kate gives her daughter a kiss on the head and runs her hand down to cup her chin. "Be good."

"I'm always good, Mummy," the little girl says with an endearing smile.

"We'll be fine, Mrs. Reynolds. You guys have a great time and don't worry about us." I wrap an arm around Susie's shoulder and she presses her cheek against my side.

With one last look, Kate rushes out the door to the car waiting out front. Her husband is always in a hurry and I've never once seen him say a kind word to little Susie. They make an odd couple, but I guess the saying is true; opposites attract.

Pushing the door closed, I turn to Susie with a smile. "So, what do you want to do?"

"How about a tea party?" she suggests, her eyes twinkling with mirth.

"Sure thing, kiddo. Lead the way." I follow her up the stairs and to her room where there's a small round table already set up with a teapot and cups and saucers. Her teddy-bears all sit around the table, as if waiting for her return, and she quickly shoos them away to make room for me.

She adopts a posh accent, lifting the teapot between finger and thumb. "Tea?"

"Why thank you, ma'am. Don't mind if I do." I hold my cup out for her to fill, expecting nothing but air, but crystal clear water pours from the spout.

Susie takes a seat opposite me, her hands clasped in front of her.

"You're not having any tea?" I ask, lifting the cup to my lips.

"Not yet. I like mine to steep longer."

I chuckle, wondering how many real life tea parties she's attended to know to let it steep. With puckered lips, I pretend to take a sip, and she frowns.

"You're doing it wrong. You have to hold your pinkie out, like this." She lifts the cup in front of her, one dainty finger sticking out to the side. "And you have to drink it for real."

"My apologies. I didn't realise there was an etiquette to uphold."

She smiles, nodding her head as if she's used to having to explain herself. "We are ladies, and there is always an etiquette."

"Yes. Right. Of course." I lower my cup back onto the saucer, spinning it around so the rose print is facing me. "These are pretty." In fact, the whole set up is rather incredible. Each piece is made of China, with a different flower painted on the front, and a gold edge runs around the rim. They wouldn't look out of place at a proper high tea event.

"That one is my favourite." Susie points at the one in front of me.

"I'm honoured you'd let me use it."

"You're my favourite babysitter," she says by way of explanation, and a warm glow settles in my chest. "I wish you could stay and play more often."

"I'm sure that could be arranged."

Her eyes light up, and she sits a little taller in her seat. "That would be grand. Mummy is always too busy with Daddy to play with me for long."

"Oh, I'm sure she would play with you more if you asked her."

Susie's eyes darken. "No, she wouldn't."

There's a ping from my pocket, and I pull my phone out, glancing at the screen.

Susie folds her arms, a scowl on her face. "No phones at the table, young lady."

I quickly respond to Braden with the address and tuck my phone away. "Sorry, I should know better. Not ladylike behaviour, is it?"

Susie smooths her hands across the table. "No, it's not. It's rude. Who was it, anyway?"

"Oh." I wave my hand through the air. "Just my boyfriend. He's coming by later to do some homework with me after you go to bed."

"You're not allowed to have boys here."

"It's okay, I already checked with your mum. She's fine with it."

Susie pushes up from the table, stomps over to the door and pushes it closed with a click. "*I'm* not fine with it."

A shiver runs down my spine as an icy breeze seems to come out of nowhere. "Do you have a window open in here?" I glance around, rubbing my hands up and down my arms for warmth. "It's so cold."

Susie stands beside me, lifting my cup of 'tea' and bringing it to my lips. "This will warm you up."

I push her hand away. "No thank you. I think I'm done with the tea party." Bracing my hands on the table, I make to stand, but Susie pushes me back down with a hand to my shoulder. She's surprisingly strong for a seven-year-old.

"The tea party isn't finished until I say it is." She leans down, an inch from my face. Her lips twist into a disturbing smile, stretching wider than should be possible. "Drink up."

"I don't—"

"I said drink!" She shoves the cup against my mouth, the China edge cutting into my lip. Cool liquid seeps onto my tongue, and when I try to cry out, there's no sound. I stare at her with wide eyes, my heart pounding in my chest.

Susie runs a hand down my hair, and I pull away, trying desperately to tell her to stop whatever this is, but my voice won't cooperate. My mouth opens and closes like a fish out of water as my hands glide over my throat, my chin, my lips.

"It won't work. You're mine now." She skips around to the other side of the table and takes her seat. Beside me, another girl around my age, gives me a sympathetic smile. She takes my hand and points to the mirror across the room. There, in the reflection, is the small table set up for the tea party, and where the teddy-bears once sat, there's now the girl and me, and we're smiling and drinking the tea along with Susie.

I look down at my hands in my lap then back to the mirror where I'm laughing and taking another sip of tea. I don't understand what I'm seeing. It's impossible, and yet, there I am, playing along.

There's a knock on the door, drawing my attention away from the mirror, and a new sliver of fear takes hold.

Braden.

I clumsily push away from the table, racing for the door to warn him, but the door is locked and I don't have a key. Susie steps past me, opening the door with ease and closing it behind her. I pound my hands on the wood until it shakes in its frame, but to no avail. Footsteps climb the stairs; two sets. One small, dainty-footed person, and one heavy-footed.

I kick the door, rattle the doorknob, but it's no use. Braden steps through with Susie's hand clasped in his. He smiles at reflection me and joins her at the table, while I sit silently beside him, trying to reach him. I tug his hair, scratch a nail down his cheek, shake his shoulders.

Nothing.

Susie gives me that same evil grin, her lips curling almost to her ears as she offers him a cup of tea. Tears course down my face as I watch him take a sip, knowing we'll both be stuck forever, but there's nothing I can do about it.

Only, Braden's reflection doesn't change, and he doesn't lose his voice. Instead, he clutches at his throat, gasping for breath. He topples sideways, knocking the table and chairs across the room as his face goes redder and redder. His eyes bulge, and spittle forms at the corner of his lips. With one last kick of his legs, he goes still, his hands limp against his chest.

I open my mouth to scream, but still no sound comes out. Crawling over to him, I beat a fist against his chest, willing him to live, to breathe, to fight. It's no use. My hands don't seem to connect, and when I look up at the mirror, his reflection begins to fade.

Susie takes her seat again, pouring more tea into our cups. "I told you. No boys allowed."

I honestly can't tell you where this one came from. My best guess is it was a dream. I was scrolling through my phone one day, clearing notes, when I stumbled across this very detailed note about a little girl witch who convinced people to drink her potions and trapped them. I changed a few pieces, because some of it was vague, but I had fun trying to turn it into something legible.

A Note from the Author

Thank you so much for taking the time to read my collection of short stories and poems. I hope you enjoyed them. If you did, I would love for you to leave a review on your favourite platform, or even share it with your friends. Word of mouth is the best way for our books to be seen.

If you would like to keep up to date on my releases, feel free to sign up to my newsletter. I promise, I will not spam you! On sign up, you will receive a link to a FREE ecopy of a short holiday romance I wrote.

http://eepurl.com/cULu_f

Thanks again!
Stacey xxx

Acknowledgements

To the people who approach me in the supermarket to ask about my books, thank you. To those who recognise me by my laugh or a post they've seen on social media, thank you. It honestly makes my day when you reach out to me. It can be a lonely job writing, and to have someone acknowledge you when you least expect it can mean so much. I have always said that I write for myself; writing the stories I want to read, but I also write for you.

To Trina, one of my closest friends and proofreader/editor extraordinaire, I adore you. You've been by my side from the beginning, and I couldn't have done it without you. I miss our weekly coffees!

To Indi, Debs, and Nicole, my writing buddies who continually check in on me to see how I'm getting on, thank you. It's been a slow few months, but I finally feel as though I'm clawing my way back, so thank you for being there throughout and encouraging me.

And to all the readers out there who take a chance on indie authors, thank you! Writing without you would not be anywhere near as fun and satisfying. Every review or share is very much appreciated, and I read them all. Thank you, thank you, thank you xxx

Connect With Me

www.staceybroadbent.com/

www.facebook.com/StaceyBroadbentAuthor

Broadbent's Bookish Babes: https://goo.gl/FY9wQN

www.amazon.com/author/staceybroadbent

Goodreads: https://goo.gl/YJ6dXa

www.instagram.com/authorstaceybroadbent/

www.bookbub.com/authors/stacey-broadbent

www.tiktok.com/@authorstaceybroadbent

Other Books by Stacey Broadbent

Standalone
Never Judge a Book
Emma
Deep Heat
Lady Luck: A Deep Heat bonus novella
Fever
A Christmas Tail

A Step in Time series
Dancing through the Storm
Dancing in Circles
Dancing with Destiny
A Step in Time: the complete series

Super Mum series
Frazzled
Frazzled and Frumpy
Frazzled, Frumpy and Fabulous!
Super Mum: the complete series

Dark sins novellas
Sins of the Flesh
Mine

Hellhounds MC series
Cut Loose
Break Loose

Short Stories and Poetry
Musings, Mournings, and Misadventures
Musings, Mayhem, and Mystery
Musings, Magic, and Mischief

Anthologies
Scars to your Beautiful
Witching Hour: Vices and Virtues
The White Ribbon Collection
Key to my Heart
A Touch of Inspiration
No Place Like Home
Serendipity
Lucky Star
Hellhounds
Hiraeth

Stacey resides in Ashburton, New Zealand with her husband and three children. She is a qualified proofreader, author, wife, mother, and self-proclaimed culinary goddess. When she's not busy writing or editing books, she enjoys reading and procrastinating on TikTok.

She absolutely loves hearing from readers, so please feel free to reach out via email, Instagram, or join her reader group, Broadbent's Bookish Babes.

www.staceybroadbent.com